歌集

若葉のささやき
Whisper of young leaves

松井純代
Matsui Sumiyo

本阿弥書店

歌集　若葉のささやき＊目次

陽だまりの動物たち　5
Animals in the sunshine

明日香から吹く風　15
The wind from Asuka

美しい山河　25
Beautiful mountains and rivers

春のそよ風　37
Spring breeze

初夏の光　45
Summer light

静かな日々に　51
Quiet days

塾の毎日　59
Daily life at juku school

家族の声　73
The voice of my family

光の中で　81
In the light

イギリスへの旅　89
The trip to England

afterword　　　　　Dan Parsons　96
あとがき　　　　　　松井　純代　98

装幀　巖谷純介

歌集
若葉のささやき
Whisper of young leaves

松井 純代

Dan Parsons

陽だまりの動物たち

Animals in the sunshine

ななかまど　赤く色づき　白き犬
　　ひたすら眠る　陽だまりの中

Rowan trees turn red
A white dog is sleeping soundly
in the sunshine

かたまりて　水仙の咲く　線路わき
　ゆくりと歩き　ゆく黒き猫

Lines of narcissi bloom
along the railway tracks
A black cat is walking slowly

待ちわびし　ヤモリ出でこず　月の夜
　　いずこで深く　眠りているや

I waited for a longtime
but the gecko doesn't appear tonight
I wonder where it's sleeping
in the moonlight

Ｓの字の　群れゆるやかに　崩れきて
　　鳥たち夕陽の　ビルに降り立つ

A flock of birds form an "S"
with their flight
The letter crumbles and lands
on a building in the evening light

冬枯れの　芝生の上の　黒き猫
　　　陽だまりの中で　長きあくびす

On the withering lawn
A black cat yawns lazily in the sunshine

人参の　かけらのそばで　コクリコと
　　ウサギ居眠る　陽だまりの小屋

Next to some morsels of carrot
A rabbit is nodding off
in its cage in the sunshine

なにもかも　わかりたるよな　眼を持ちし
　　ウサギゆきたり　粉雪がふる

Her eyes showed me
that she could read my heart
When my rabit passed
the snow fell gently

真夜中の　屋根裏世界が　あるような
　　イタチがネズミを　追いかける音

Other worldly in the attic at midnight
The sound of a weasel chasing a mouse

明日香から吹く風
The wind from Asuka

ふるさとは　小高い丘の　上にあり
　　えんどうの花　白く咲きたり

My hometown upon its gentle hill
Now covered in white pea blossom

サギ一羽　眺める川面　ゆったりと
　　花びら寄せて　飛鳥川ゆく

A heron stands watching
the surface of the river
Petals float down the Asuka-gawa

大きなる　亀石の横を　川流る
　　小さく咲きたる　きつねのボタン

A great stone turtle by the stream
Tiny yellow flowers
called fox buttons blossom

新緑に　包まれはるか　石舞台
　　二弦の箏の　古曲流れる

Thoughts of bygone times
Ishibutai is covered with fresh leaves
A two-string koto plsys ancient melodies

弟と　許嫁とが　登りゆく
　　柿の若葉の　持統陵へと

My brother and his fiancé climb up
the mausoleum of emperor Zito
Through the young persimmon leaves

二上山は　茜に染まり　稲刈りを
　　終えて野を焼く　煙漂う

Mt. Futakami turns dark red
After the harvest the rice fields are burned
The smoke is billowing

飛鳥川　瀬音も立てず　子供らは
　　　川辺の石を　拾いて投げる

Asuka-gawa flows quietly
Children pick up pebbles
and throw them into the river

花明かり　淡く包めり　いつしかに
　　盛土なくせし　馬子の墓を

Ancient tomb of Umako Soga is covered with
the pale brightness of cherry blossom
The soil of the tomb was lost
a long time ago

＊蘇我馬子の墓は盛土がなくなり、巨大な石組みだけが残り、
　石舞台古墳として明日香のシンボルとなっています

美しい山河

Beautiful mountains and rivers

大き弧を　空に描きし　飛行機雲
　　畑にたわわな　青き梅の実

A Jet flies drawing a big arc in the sky
Green Japanese apricots cover the field

菜の花の　続く岸辺を　かたむきて
　　グライダー飛ぶ　光をうけて

Rape blossoms stretch along the bank
A glider leans to reflect the sun

水張田に　マンションの灯の　映りたり
　青く輝く　蛍火のごと

Rice fields are full of water
Lights from the apartment block
reflect brightly like fireflies

山しょうの　若芽を食みて　育ちたる
　　アゲハ羽化せる　梅雨明けの空

　Swallowtail caterpillars ate the leaves of
　a young Japanese pepper tree
　Butterflies emerge as sky clear
　End of the rainy season

風が好き　風に揺れたる　クモの巣も
　　　夏の空ゆく　ジェット機もまた

I like wind, spiders' webs moving
in the breeze
and jets flying in the summer sky

色づきし　麦が大地を　切り分ける
　　　パッチワークの　丘広がりぬ

Wheat yellowing in the spring wind
Colourful patchworks cover the hills

大叔父が　開墾せしとう　北の大地
　　　はるかに白く　蕎麦の花咲く

Far from where we live
My great uncle reclaimed
the northern lands
Small white buckwheats blossom
in the distance

馬鈴薯と　もろこし畑の　丘の上に
　　焦点のごと　赤い小屋あり

Potato and cornfields spread across the hill
Focus on a hut with a red roof

魂が　戻り来るような　闇の中
　　蛍舞いたり　明日香の棚田

The darkness returns like a spirit
Many fireflies are flying
over the terraced fields in Asuka

けものらの　浅き眠りを　呼び起こす
　　柿色の月　出でし香具山

Many animals are sleeping
Full moon is rising over Mt. Kaguyama
They are awakened by the beautiful moon

春のそよ風

Spring breeze

えんどうを　摘む人白き　花の中
　　遠く光れる　ソーラーパネル

Among the white flowers
A man is picking string beans
Solar panels shine in the distance

庭隅に　幼き日々を　見つけたり
　からすのえんどう　すずめのてっぽう

I remember my childhood
when I find these little plants
"crow's beans" and "sparrow's gun"

若草を　踏みつつ進む　赤や黄の
　傘の行列　畦道をゆく

Children walk on the path
between the rice fields
Their red and yellow umbrellas make
a colourful procession

「こうもりが飛んでいたよ」といいし子と
　休耕田を　しばし眼で追う

"A bat flew by" said the child
For a while I look across
the resting rice field

ポロロンと　忘れたころに　オルゴール
　音ひとつたて　やがてしずけし

When I forgot about the musical box
It suddenly makes a sound
only to fall silent again

靴ひもが　固く結ばれ　片方が
　　　転がり残る　街路樹の下

A discarded shoe lies
under a roadside tree
The lace is tied tightly

初夏の光
Summer light

甘き香を　残し自転車　こぎゆくむすめ
　　水玉模様の　パラソル揺らし

A girl cycles past me
leaving a sweet fragrance
Her polka-dot parasol is trembling

蛍狩り　水の中にて　光れるは
　　蛇の目なると　子等はいいあう

Off to hunt fireflies
"Those shiny points of light in the water
are snakes'eyes" The children say

クーラーの　音せせらぎと　聞こえきて
魚となりゆく　疲れし体

I hear the sound of the air conditioner
like the song of a stream
My tired body becomes a fish

営業マン　石のベンチに　腰掛けて
　　彫塑となりぬ　駅前広場

A salesman is sitting on a stone bench
He looks like a statue
in the square in front of the station

静かな日々に
Quiet days

ハヤブサが　やがて大きなムササビと
　　なりて降り立つ　ジャンプの着地

A falcon becomes a giant flying squirrel
descends and lands at the bottom
of the ski jump

ある時は　両の手相を　眺めいる
　　　未来の声を　聞きとるように

Once, wanting to know the future
I carefully compared both my palms
to hear the voice of the future

わが部屋の　幾百冊の　本なべて
　　　記憶の森の　いずこに消えし

Many hundred of books in my room
They may be hidden in the forest
of my memory

見つむれば　吸い寄せられて　いくような
　　夜をてらせる　青き信号

Staring at the traffic signal at night
I am sucked forward by the green light

目に見えぬ　円を描きて　ここよりは
　　出でぬときめし　長き歳月

Imagining an invisible circle around me
I decided not to leave it for a long time

眠られぬ　夜に眺める　屏風絵の
　　谷間の川の　流れゆく先

When I can't sleep at night
I gaze at the river flowing from the valley
painted on my folding screen
I wonder where it goes

塾の毎日

Daily life at juku school

子供らは　冷たい風の　かたまりと
　　なりてきたりぬ　如月の夜

Students enter
like a gust of cold north wind
one February night

夜汽車ゆく　汽笛の響き　寂しかり
　　板書をしつつ　静かに聞けり

A night train's lonely whistle sounds
I listen quietly while writing
on the blackboard

教室の　曇りガラスを　手で拭う
　　遠き駅舎の　あかり輝く

I wipe the classroom's misty window
with my hand
The distant station's lights shine brightly

部活終え　来たれる子らが　口々に
　　今夜は星が　きれいだという

The students arrive after their club activities
They tell me in unison
"The stars are beautiful tonight"

受験生　窓に乗り出し　つぶやきぬ
　　　「こんどは鳥に　生まれてきたい」

Opening the window an examinee student
looks at the sky mumbling
"I'd like to be born as a bird in my next life"

教室の柱に「みんなありがとう」
　　落書き残し　子は越していく

On a pillar in the classroom
"Thank you everyone"
A message left by a student
who moved away

柔らかい　子らの心に　癒されて
　　今宵静かに　授業を終えぬ

Warmed by the tender heart
of one student
I finish the class smoothly tonight

如月の　空の青さの　中にたつ
　　受験する子の　静かな闘志

An examinee student stands against
a blue February sky
He is calm with the spirit of endeavor

降り続く　夜更けの雪を　語りつつ
　　講師ら山の　奥へと帰る

After the class teachers talk about
the midnight snowfall
They'll go home deep into the mountains

生徒らの　合否の電話　待つ窓辺
　　　パキラの小さき　若葉が伸びる

I wait for my students'phone calls about
their examination results
A young pachira is growing
by the window

ガラス窓に　浮かびしヤモリは
　　柿色の　月にはめられし　銀の象嵌

A gecko on the glass at night
Appears like a silver inlay
on the orange full moon

教室を　閉めて出づれば　夜の木々は
　　枝を広げて　切り絵のごとし

When I leave the classroom at night
The branches of the trees in the field
look like a paper cut-out picture

家族の声

The voice of my family

数年を　くらせしのみの　母の歌
　　かすかに覚ゆ　春風の中

Only a few years spent together
I faintly remember my mother singing
in the spring breeze

放課後に　長く別れし　母がきて
　　物言わざりし　十五の私

Mother lived far away for a long time
but came to see me after school one day
I said nothing
I was fifteen

八歳で　別れし母に　添い寝する
　　病棟の夜の　深き静けさ

Separated at the age of eight
Now I sleep near my mother's bed
It's quiet in the hospital at night

わが病めば　逝きにし父が　そばに来て
　気遣いくれし　朝方の夢

When I was sick
My father came to take care of me
in my early morning dream
Though he passed many years ago

過ぎしこと　包みてふりぬ　春の雪
　　　義母逝きてまだ　日の浅き午後

The snow on a spring afternoon
covers the past
My mother-in-law passed a few month ago

子に道を　強いてはならぬ　思いあり
　空に傾く　白き月みゆ

I think I must not force my child
to follow my path
In the sky I see the white moon

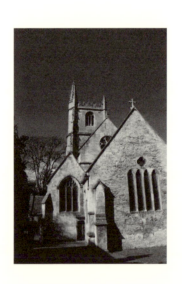

光の中で
In the light

人流る　広きホームの　片隅で
　　彫塑のように　警備員立つ

People stream through the station
A guard stands in a corner
as still as a statue

葉の落ちし　高き木の枝　ゆがみたり
　　魔女の手のごと　天と地を指す

The leaves have fallen from the tall tree
The twisting branches point
to the heaven and the earth
like a witch's fingers

冬の空　身の引き締まるほど　澄み渡り
　　大志持ちたる　若き日思う

The clear winter sky
My body becomes taut when I look up
I remember youthful days full of ambition

笑わない　少年に似し　三日月が
　　葉桜の上で　光り始める

The new crescent moon begins to shine
over the leaves of the cherry trees
like a boy that never laughs

思い出の　二つ三つほど　携えて
　　いずこにゆきし　青き扇子は

I wonder where my blue fan is
　There are a few of my memories in it

湖底に　あまたの土器を　眠らせて
　　水は千年　流れてゆきぬ

Under the soil of the lake bed
Lie countless pieces of earthenware
The water has flowed for a thousand years

天武天皇・持統天皇・元明天皇などが都城した藤原宮跡（694年から710年）の横に大きい醍醐池があります。池の底にたくさんの土器が埋もれていました

イギリスへの旅
The trip to England

春浅く　羊草食む　なだらかな
　　丘を越えゆき　カンタベリーへ

In early spring
Sheep are eating grass
as I cross the low hill to Cantabery

ドーバー海峡より　吹きくる風をうけており
　　白亜の絶壁　セブンシスター

Wind blowing from the straits of Dover
hits the chalky Seven Sisters

カモメ舞う　ライの駅前　静かなり
　　エニシダ咲きし　中世の町

Seagulls fly around the station at Rye
Yellow flowers blossom in a medieval town

広大な　グリーングラスの　丘続き
　　　ストーンヘンジの　ふいにあらわる

A wide hill was covered with green grass
Suddenly Stonehenge appears

バイブリー　蜂蜜色の 壁続く
　　絵本のような　小さい村に

The village of Bibury
A myriad of honey-colored cottages
stretch out like a picture book

テームズ河の　速き流れに　乗りて見る
　　夕陽に染まる　ロンドンの街

The river Thames flow fast
Watching from a boat
I see the sunset over London town

afterword

Originally from Bristol in England, I have been resident in Japan for almost half a century, living most of that time in Nara prefecture.

Matsui san has been a dedicated English language student of mine for many years, so when she first suggested the idea of creating a book of bilingual tanka, I jumped at the chance to help.

The task was quite challenging; considering all of the hidden meanings and inferences contained within tanka, not to mention the syllabic restrictions.
Finally, it was decided to forego the syllable count in favour of recreating the feeling of each piece in English as closely as possible to the original Japanese. This in itself still proved to be difficult. However, Matsui san and I feel that the end results are relatively close in character to the source material, so we hope that you can enjoy these verses in both languages.

Dan Parsons.

あとがき

　私は、イギリスのブリストルの出身で、ほとんど半世紀近く日本に居住しています。その大部分を奈良県で暮らしてきました。
　松井さんは長年にわたる私の英語教室の生徒です。彼女が最初に二か国語の短歌の本を作るという考えを提案した時、私は、手助けをする機会に飛び乗りました。
　その作業はとても大変でした。なぜなら、韻律に制限があるのはいうまでもなく、短歌に含まれる隠された意味や暗喩をすべて考えなければならなかったからです。
　最終的には、韻律にとらわれることを控えて、各作品の感情を元の日本語にできるだけ近い形で再現することにしました。これ自体まだなお難しいことでした。
　しかし、松井さんと私は最終的にできあがったものは、その短歌のもとの感情に比較的近いものになったと感じています。
　そして、私達は読者の皆さんに両方の言語で短歌を楽しんでいただくことを願っています。

　　2018年8月　　　　　　　　　　Dan Parson（訳・松井）

あとがき

　私は、田舎で小さい学習塾を開いています。主に中学生と一緒に毎日を過ごしています。私の趣味の一つであります短歌を英語で表しますと子供たちはどのような反応をしてくれるのかなと思い、英語で短歌の作品をまとめることにしました。
　情景がすぐにわかるような作品を選びました。そして、中学生のわかる易しい英語で表現してみました。文法的にそぐわない部分があるとおもいますが、短歌に照らして読んでいただきたいと思います。子供たちが短歌の楽しさと英語のおもしろさを味わってくれることをねがいます。
　英語の翻訳に際しまして長く英会話教室で教えてくださり、いつも楽しく導いてくださるDan先生に見て頂き、アドバイスをして頂きました。ありがとうございました。また最後にDan先生のふるさとのイギリスを旅した折の歌をいれました。子供たちが短歌や英語に興味を持ってくれますことをねがっております。
　出版に際しまして本阿弥書店さんにお世話になりましたこと感謝申し上げます。お蔭様で出版の運びとなりましたこと大変うれしく思っております。ありがとうございました。

　2018年8月

　　　　　　　　　　　　　　　　　　　松井純代

著者略歴

松井純代（まつい　すみよ）

1949年　奈良県高市郡明日香村生まれ
1998年　「日月」入会
　　　　学習塾経営
2014年　歌集『夜の教室』刊

現住所　〒634-0072
　　　　奈良県橿原市醍醐町105-10

訳者略歴

Dan Parsons

1962年　イギリス、Bristol 生まれ
1994年　来日
　　　　英語教師
住　所　奈良県香芝市

歌集　若葉のささやき

2018年10月21日

著　者　松井　純代
定　価　1600円（税別）
発行者　奥田　洋子
発行所　本阿弥書店
　　　　東京都千代田区神田猿楽町2-1-8　三恵ビル　〒101-0064
　　　　電話　03-3294-7068（代）　　　振替00100-5-164430

印刷・製本　日本ハイコム㈱

ISBN978-4-7768-1398-9（3114）　Printed in Japan
Ⓒ Matsui Sumiyo 2018